THE SAME INSIDE

By Trevor Witchey

DORRANCE
PUBLISHING CO
EST 1920
PITTSBURGH PENNSYLVANIA 15235

Dorrance Publishing Co
585 Alpha Drive
Pittsburgh, PA 15238
Visit our website at www.dorrancebookstore.com

ISBN: 978-1-6393-7288-1
eISBN: 978-1-6393-7686-5

THE SAME INSIDE

By Trevor Witchey

Breathe, breathe in the air...
No matter who you are or where you come
from, each of us has a similar pair of lungs.

We are all breathing the same air,
and the wind shall flow freely through our
hair.

Mosquitos, ticks, and other insects do not see differences between us when they take aim,
because to them, all of our blood tastes the same.

For bugs, they do not care what you look
like or if you are neat,
they are just looking for a tasty treat!

Oh no! Ice cream headache!
Each of us ate ice cream too fast,
and now we are all suffering from head
pain that will last.

Our bodies are warm naturally and not meant
to quickly consume cold,
but when we do, the dreaded ice cream
headache will unfold.

Within us, we have skeletons that provide us with similar structure and shape, but if you break a bone, the doctor will give you casting tape.

Accidents can happen to anyone, and waiting for your bones to heal is not fun. But hey, your friends can sign your cast for memories that will last.

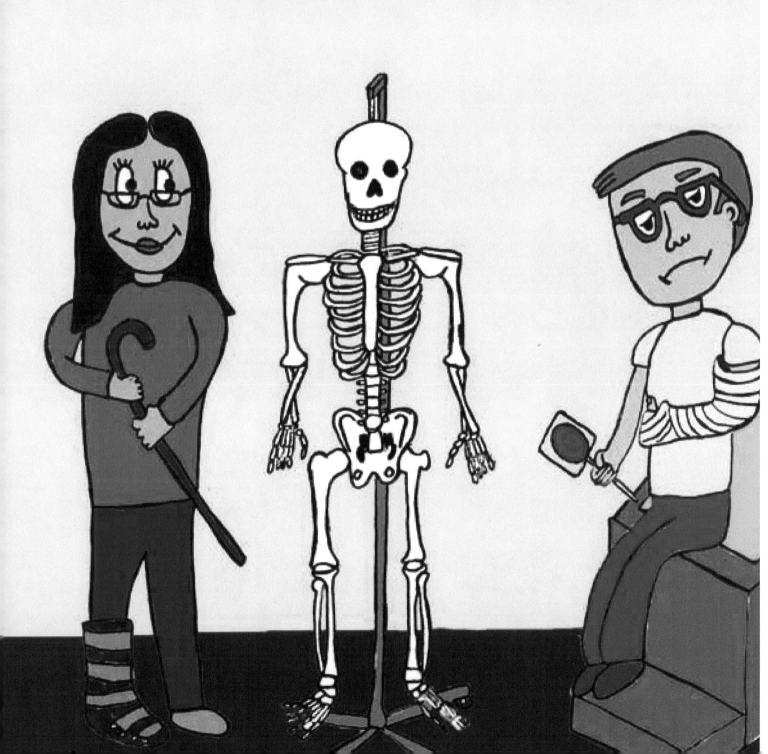

We each have a heart that pumps the same color blood throughout our bodies, while also having a heart will make us care about somebody.

With each heartbeat, we are alive and well. When we work together as a team, we can create many great stories to tell.

Donating blood is an honorable thing to do. With the right blood type, I can transfer mine to you.

Everyone has the same red blood flowing through them like a river.
When you donate, you never know whose life it could save when delivered.

Most of us have two pairs of eyes, and
despite the color and the shape,
they allow us to see the world's landscape.

While our eyes can spot differences among us, having the ability to look inward of a person is a plus.

Our nervous systems are the same and can deliver such pain.

Whether you step on something, smash your thumb, get your hand stuck in a door, or touch something with heat...

Thanks to our similar nervous systems, our bodies tell us that these events should not be repeated.

It is time to exercise and build strong muscles!
We all have a muscular system inside of us that provides great strength and ability.

When you work out often, that will greatly help out your mobility.

We are so sick! We have caught some form
of illness or virus.

Everyone has an immune system that tries
its best to protect us against viruses and
disease.

To obtain help, we see the doctor so that they may apply their expertise to put us at ease.

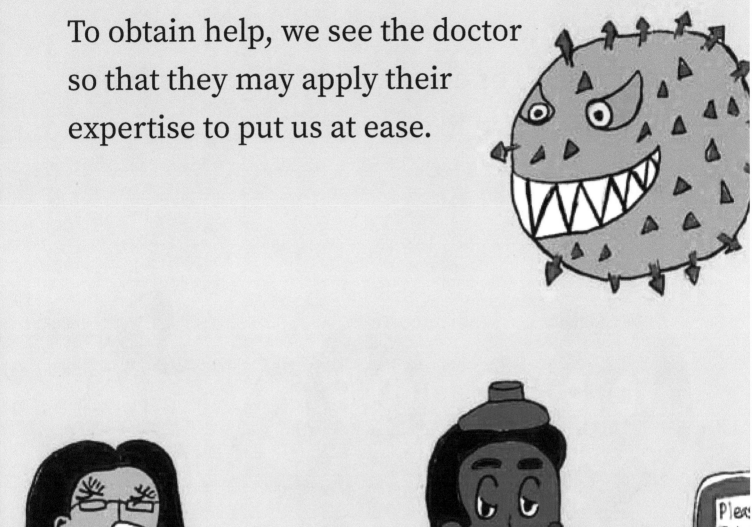

You must take care of your teeth inside of your mouth or else cavities will cause your mouth's health to go south.

Each of us has a set of teeth that help us eat or smile,
but if you do not take care of your teeth, the dentist will see you for a while.

Oh no! We ate too much pizza!
While consuming many pieces of pizza may seem delicious, the damage done to each of our digestive systems could be malicious.

Our bellies can only hold so much, as eating too much of a good thing will cause nausea or acid reflux.

It doesn't matter who you are or what you think, to a Zombie, your brains equally taste like sausage links!

Kidneys inside of us act as a filtering system
to remove toxins and waste,
but did you know that they can be replaced?

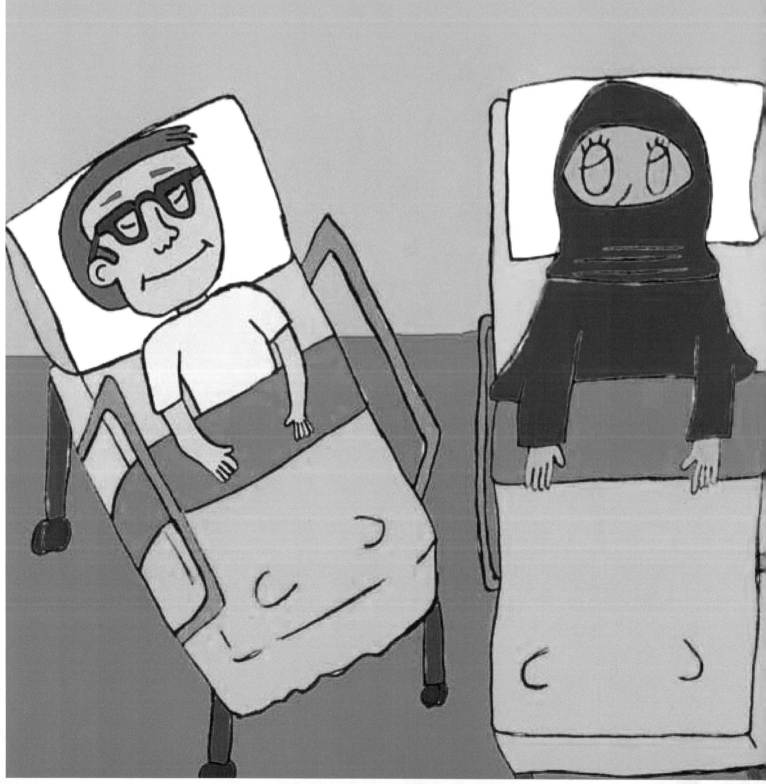

Everyone has a pair of kidneys but only needs one to survive.
By donating one of your kidneys to help someone in need, you'll help them thrive.

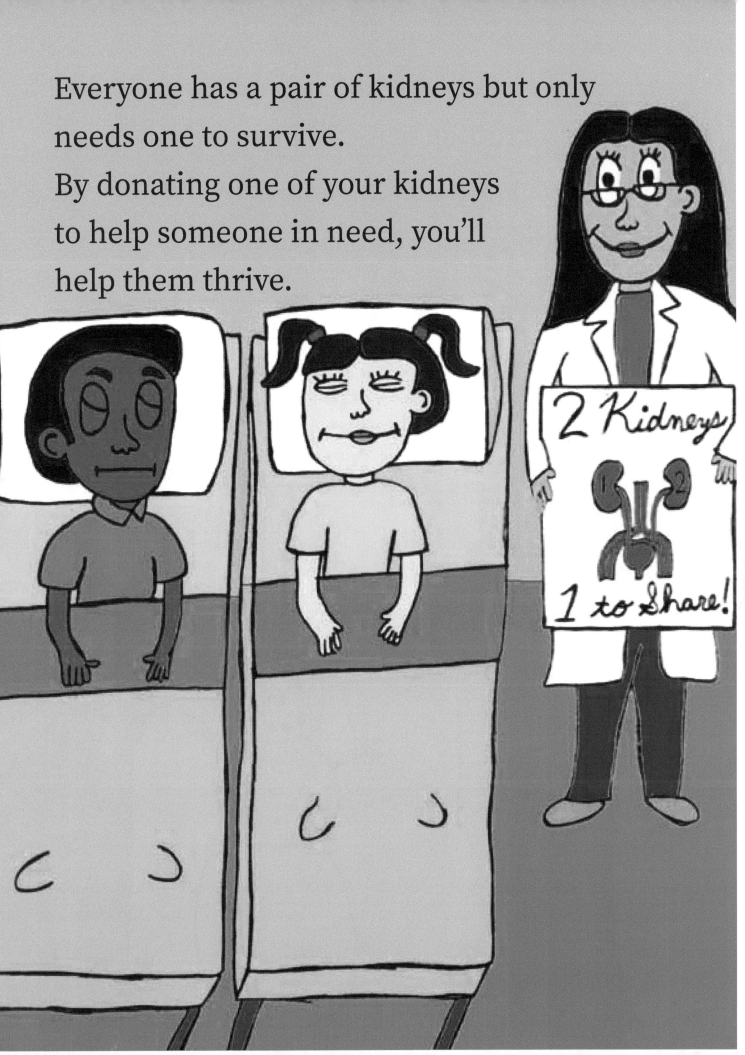

Yummy! Hot chocolate on a cold winter day! Be careful, because it will burn each of our mouths if you drink it too quickly and you do not delay.

Drinking hot chocolate and playing in the snow together are memories that we can share always and forever.

From our journey, we discovered
that many similarities were uncovered.

Inside, we're all the same
contrary to what appears on the outside or our name.

From the air we breathe to the blood our heart pumps,
disliking someone's outward appearance or lifestyle
makes you a grump!

There is plenty of this world to enjoy and see.
By overlooking diffences, we can all be free.

CPSIA information can be obtained
at www.ICGtesting.com
Printed in the USA
BVHW010733261222
654950BV00018B/159